Margret Rey

Pretzel

With Pictures by H. A. Rey

Houghton Mifflin Company
Boston 1997

Library of Congress Cataloging-in-Publication Data

Rey, Margret.
  Pretzel / by Margret Rey ; illustrated by H.A. Rey.
    p. cm.
  Summary: Pretzel finds that being the longest dachshund in all
the world is not enough to win the favor of Greta, the little dachs-
hund from across the street.
    RNF ISBN 0-395-83737-5   PAP ISBN 0-395-83733-2
    [1. Dogs — Fiction.]   I. Rey, H. A. (Hans Augusto),
1898-1977 ill. II. Title.
PZ7.R3302Pr 1997   96-9669
[E] — dc20   CIP
                       AC

Printed in the United States of America

WOZ 10 9 8 7 6 5 4 3 2 1

One morning in May five
little dachshunds were born.

Pretzel

One of them was Pretzel.
They grew up the way puppies do, and they
all looked exactly alike the first few weeks.

Paul

Patricia

Priscilla

Percival

But after nine weeks Pretzel suddenly
started growing—
              and growing—
                    and growing.

He grew much longer than
any of his brothers and sisters.

And when he was fully grown
he had become the longest
dachshund in all the world.

Pretzel was very pleased with
himself because it is very distinguished
for a dachshund to be so long.

When he was one year old (a dachshund is grown up at that age) he won the Blue Ribbon at the Dog Show which means that everybody considered him the best looking dog of all.

All the dogs admired him.
And all the people admired him.

Only Greta didn't.

Greta was the little dachshund from
across the street. Pretzel was in love
with her and wanted to marry her.

But Greta just laughed at him.
  "I don't care for long dogs," she said.
  "But it is very distinguished
for a dachshund to be so long
and I won the Blue Ribbon at the
Dog Show," said Pretzel.
  "I still don't care," said Greta.
Pretzel was hurt but he did not show it.
  "Please marry me," he said,

"and I will do anything for you!"

"Prove it!" said Greta and went away.

So Pretzel set out to prove it. First
he brought Greta a nice big bone.

"Thanks for the bone," said Greta,
"but I won't marry you for that.
I don't care for long dogs." And
she ate the bone and forgot about
Pretzel.

Pretzel had to try something else. He gave her the lovely green rubber ball he had been given for his birthday.

"Thank you," said Greta, "but I still

won't marry you because I don't care for long dogs. Besides, everybody can give *presents!*" And she ran away with the ball.

"Look what I can do! Nobody except me can do THAT!" said Pretzel when they met again.

And this is what he did:

"Not bad," said Greta. "Your name certainly fits you. But I like the pretzels at the baker's better, and I still don't care for long dogs." Pretzel was very unhappy.

Some weeks had passed and Greta hadn't even spoken to Pretzel. One day while she was playing with her green ball it bounced away. Greta tried to catch it and boomps! they both landed in a hole.

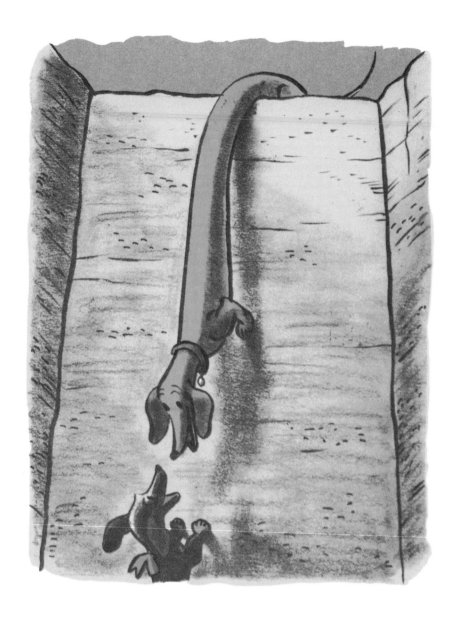

"I'll get you out of there!" he shouted.
(He had watched Greta all the time

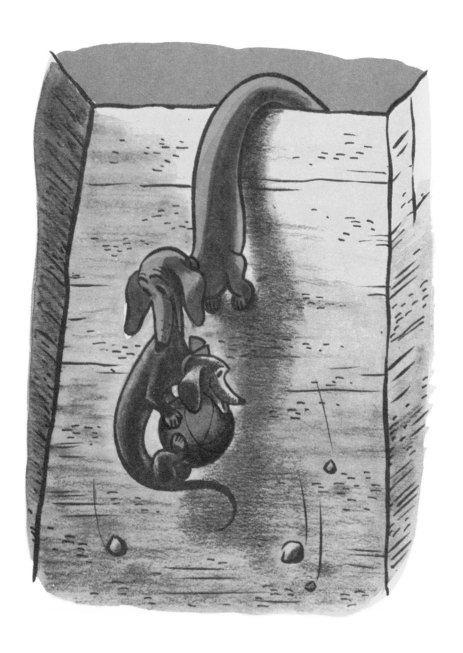

and now had rushed to help her.)
How good that Pretzel was so long!

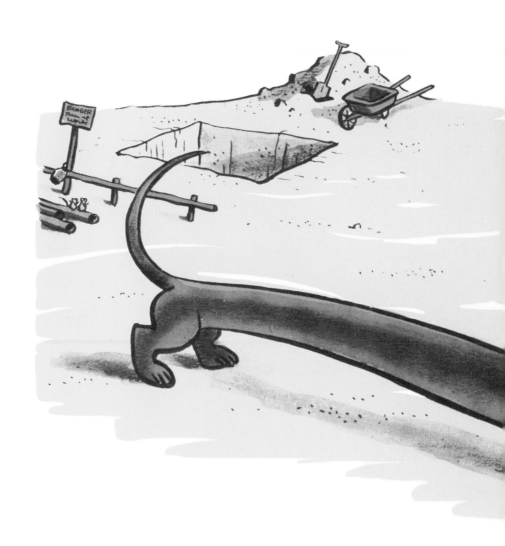

"I believe you saved my life. You are wonderful!" said Greta with a sigh.

"Will you marry me now?" asked Pretzel.
"I will," said Greta, "but not for your
length!" So they kissed each other,

and got married,

and one morning in May
five little dachshunds were born . . .